I0536658

Bouquet

Bonnie Ferrante

ISBN 978-0-9880530-0-7

ALL RIGHTS RESERVED

Copyright Bonnie Ferrante

This book may not be reproduced or used in whole or in part by any existing means without written permission from the author

This book is a work of fiction and any resemblance to persons, living or dead, or actual events is purely coincidental. The characters are products of the author's imagination and used fictitiously.

These three speculative fiction short stories were previously published in print magazines – *On Spec* and *Challenging Destiny.*

Other Books by Bonnie Ferrante

Nightfall - Dawn's End Book 1

Poisoned - Dawn's End Book 2

Outworld Apocalypse - Dawn's End Book 3

Inhale (short story collection)

Terror at White Otter Castle (novella)

Desiccate

Bouquet

I want to talk about my soul, Peter. But, to do that, I have to tell you what really happened. Judge for yourself whether I'm a traitor.

Assume this room is bugged. They still don't believe I've told them everything. I'm not sure if they let you come because you're my brother and this is my last day, or because you're a priest and I might confess I've given away federal secrets. The guard said you've been trying to see me for months. I'm sure they've sworn you to confidentiality, which you will follow.

The faithful Father Peter Baxter. Always true to the system. I prefer to be true to humanity. Humanity. Perhaps that is not the right word.

Here, have a cup of tea, Peter, and a biscuit. Get comfortable. Civilized, isn't it, even without bone china? They tend to loosen up on the last breakfast. You being a holy man doesn't hurt either, I bet. Try this jam.

Bookerman's mom sent it. It's out of this world. It's a bit seedy, but nourishing. We both need our strength, at least for the next twenty-four hours.

I know you've heard a hundred variations of the incident. Well, this is mine. We were flying south of Goose Bay. One minute I'm navigating the Vulcan, and the next I'm sitting on a soft, green floor. I didn't feel the leaving. I was there, and then I was somewhere else. There was Bookerman, Fellini, and me, your "out to make a mark" little sister. Our weapons were gone. You've seen our pictures a dozen times in the news, but if you'd seen our faces then…

Fellini freaked. Started screaming about how the air force had no fucking right to test new weapons on us without our permission. For a paranoid, he could sure be naïve. Bookerman, quiet as usual, inspected the walls and floor. He was our squadron genius with security systems.

Fellini finally stopped spitting threats and made a drawn out promise to smash a few heads when he got back. Bookerman explored every nook and cranny three times over, but it didn't look hopeful. The room was basically a box, no windows, a virtually seamless door without a handle, tiny holes in the ceiling for ventilation.

The aliens brought food and water on reed-like trays in wooden containers. They wore long gowns, like monks. Dwarfish body type. Faces hidden by large loose hoods. Fellini told us not to eat. Three aliens, three trays, three of us. Bookerman tried to jump one of our captors, but was knocked off his feet by some invisible force. They put the trays on the floor and left.

Fellini thought they were government created mutants. Too much *X-Files,* I think. He started talking about collecting our urine to drink.

I told him, "Not in this lifetime."

An hour later, the aliens returned. I'm the communications expert, so I centered out the smallest captor and gave it my most dazzling smile. No response. I stated my name, rank and serial number, and then demanded to know why we were being held prisoner. The creature nodded towards the others. I heard a low hum. It turned back to me, picked a container of water from a tray and drank. The hood fell back and I almost croaked.

Tiny black eyes. Poreless, greenish skin with dark veins. No nose. Thin lips. The ear, one long crescent shape from temple to temple. It vibrated slightly when the creature hummed and the room filled with a sweet scent. You think they're children of God, Peter? Hummers with satellite heads and floral emanation? Or, do we "have dominion" over them too?

I took the container and, against Fellini's curses, drank the water to the bottom. It was pure and cool. I really would have preferred wine. I picked up the bread.

"Put that down, Baxter," Fellini snapped.

I told him, "Go drink your piss," and took a large bite. At other times, we ate strange vegetables and grains, but nothing resembling meat.

I christened the smallest one Skywalker. I kept waiting for Darth Vader to walk in. After so many viewings of the old Jedi movies, I thought anything was possible.

Remember when Father Charles told us marriage was like a tricycle? The man was the large wheel and the woman and children were the small wheels. I thought, *screw that. I'm never getting married. I don't want to be a little back wheel forever.* Man, I thought I could fly away from all the stupid, tight, trapped little wheels. Someday the air force would let women be fighter pilots. I'd be a twenty-first centure Leia, unstoppable. At no man's mercy. Who needs wheels when you could have wings?

Finish your biscuit.

I tried languages, gestures, even Morse Code. Who knew how long they'd been hovering around earth? Then I attempted binary code, using my pointer fingers. Nothing. Finally, I sang the scale. They were mesmerized, hummed each note back to me, and then rushed out of the room. They returned shortly.

"Yes, we come in peace," said the machine in Skywalker's hand. It was a mixture of our own voices, as if they'd been taped, spliced, and played back. They couldn't form words since they didn't have the same structure of mouth, larynx, and throat. They communicated using a mixture of gestures, pitch, and scent.

I was called a *chanter*. The word *prisoner* didn't seem to have an equivalent in their culture. They'd taken us out of the Vulcan because we seemed most likely to be comfortable on their ship and we might have common experiences which would make communications easier.

I explained a few basic needs, comfort, hygiene, personal privacy. They accommodated as best they could. I felt so powerful. The mouthpiece of the world. First contact. Then, like a D-grade movie, reality gave an odd twist.

Roswell, New Mexico, the stuff of pocketbooks, came up. The Hummers wanted information about an aircraft downed in 1947. They had taken all this time to trace it and then prepare for contact.

"The Americans'll never give them back the aircraft," said Fellini.

"Keep aircraft," said Skywalker's machine. "Want beings."

"They just want their people back," whispered Bookerman.

Fellini thought the word *people* didn't apply. I looked at Skywalker. He formed a small smile.

I tried to explain that it was a different government, that we were expendable captains, that our chances were nil.

Skywalker hummed and a bitter smell filled the room.

"What if Washington says no?" I asked.

"We will not be glad."

"You will not hurt us? Cause us pain?"

"Is food not good?"

"I mean, if the Americans will not give you back your people, will you kill us?"

More humming. A scent like mango and clover. I don't think they understood the question.

I sent the message to Ottawa. Washington denied all knowledge of a downed alien air craft and ordered them to depart or else. I thought that was bloody pompous, over Canadian air space. Skywalker was confused. I explained that they were a threat to earth.

"Threat like 'smash a few heads'?"

I snorted and looked at Fellini.

Skywalker responded,"No. Not true. Unreal. Never. Negative. No threat. No harm. No weapons. Not in this lifetime."

I laughed. Fellini asked about the force field.

"The shell is to protect from harm," they explained. "We did not anticipate deliberate attempt to injure. It is unknown to us."

They took me to a separate part of the ship, to explain their systems. It was so far beyond me. I had no context. They insisted the only defense they had was a repelling shell around the ship to prevent damage. Nothing offensive. I couldn't honestly tell if it was true, so I didn't pass that on to Ottawa. One more nail in my coffin.

The men gave the other two names: Doc and Bashful. Maybe we had slipped into a fairy tale. I sent a flurry of messages to Ottawa.

"We have patience," explained Skywalker. "They will understand if we find the right words."

Each alien now had a communicator and Bookerman was deep in discussion with Doc. He was fascinated by the Hummer's music, but I think it was meaningless without the context of scent. Fellini told him repeatedly to shut up and not give information to the enemy.

Doc solved that. He showed us the audio and visual tapes they were making of radio and television broadcasts. "If we want information, it is already available," he explained.

Here, Peter, finish up the last of this jam. I've eaten all I can and I'll be damned if I'll let the guards have it.

Inevitably, the topic of the dead aliens in Roswell arose. Why did they want them back so badly?

"Life is death is life is death," said Doc. "To know and believe is to be truly alive for eternity."

I thought about you, my brother, the priest. Wouldn't you love to sink your teeth into a metaphysical discussion with an alien who'd never seen a Bible? You think the Hummers crucified a Christ? They have no concept of execution.

"But we must bring our people home," said Skywalker. "They have been removed from the garden. There is a void in our existence. We did not anticipate this risk when they volunteered to explore outside the garden."

"Yes," said Doc, "it was a mistake. Our planet hopes to regain the loss. Then there will be no more of such travel. If others choose to come to us, they will be welcome."

We exchanged glances.

"So what happens when you get the bodies back?" said Fellini.

The aliens joined hands and a glow travelled through their arms. Skywalker explained. The scent was like cinnamon and peony.

On their planet, their dead are immersed in tanks of fertilizer until decomposed. Experimental seeds from crossbred plants are then sown in this soil. The dominant vegetation is then cultivated and nurtured until the soil is exhausted and several plants are brought to seed.

The spent soil is scattered in the wild. The seeds are packaged, labeled with the dead person's identity and given out. Hummers plant these in their personal gardens. Some go to seed for the next season. This is germiliving.

Each person has a collection of seeds when they pass down through generations. They believe an energy, even a type of consciousness continues. Central garden banks keep the seeds preserved for posterity in case of a loss. "Living seeds" are stored and catalogued all over the planet.

The dead explorers locked away in Roswell had no living seeds. Doc was concerned that their tissues may have been damaged or destroyed. What would their community do? The plants grown from living seeds are believed to influence other species around them. Plants from beings of such courage, intelligence, and sacrifice would be surely beneficial to all. The demand for their living seeds would be phenomenal. How could Skywalker and the others return home empty-handed? Not only did the living cry out for their return, but the dead, trapped in limbo, were unable to germilive. How could the cycle be left broken?

I asked them what happens if a Hummer burns to death. It didn't matter. The ashes were germilived. Pretty flexible, don't you think?

Skywalker started asking me personal questions. He wanted to know the difference between me and the others. I explained that I was a woman, the sex that bore children. I asked if he was male or female; after all, the robes were fairly concealing.

"I am, we are all, both."

"No kidding. Can you have children?"

"No. We must have alien." Skywalker smiled.

They may not have ribs, but they got a funny bone.

I would never have had kids, not the marrying kind. I've had sex, absolve me if it'll make you feel better. It didn't feel like a sin. It felt like a waste of time.

You know, my first sexual encounter, I was twelve. Not what you think. Remember how I used to babysit at Johnston's? The road home was pretty dark. No one ever thought about danger, except Dad told me to watch out for bears. Wrong kind of animal. No. I wasn't raped. Just three stupid boys hiding in the bush, playing sick games. They knocked me down. One of them shoved his hand under my top and squeezed my breast.

"Damn." he laughed, "They are real."

I pushed him off and ran, faster than I've ever run before. I fell on the gravel and tore a huge hole in my brand new jeans. I'd bought them myself with babysitting money because Dad said brand names were a waste of money. The boys chased me all the way home. Dad was out. I locked the door. They ran around and banged on the windows a few times, then left. I threw the jeans out. I never told Dad. I remembered how he said girls who dress to draw attention to themselves shouldn't be surprised when they get in trouble. I still have the scar on my knee.

A couple of officers on the base have tried similar things, but they found out a second-Dan black belt is no pushover.

Communications with Ottawa dragged. Fellini got a little stir crazy. He seemed to resent the relationships Bookerman and I made with the Hummers. He finally lost it and took a swing at Bookerman, who responded in kind. Just then, the Hummers came in. They circled the two fools rolling around on the floor and started chanting, "Alarm. Alarm. Alarm." It was enough to unnerve the men; they pulled apart and stared at our keepers.

The Hummers were shocked that the men had deliberately harmed each other. The men started arguing and shouting again. When they jumped to their feet, the aliens formed a barrier between them.

Skywalker wondered if their food had caused an illness. I explained about captivity and what it does to a person. About homesickness. This they understood.

Skywalker was ashamed and promised our immediate return. Fellini whooped for joy. Everyone shook hands and expressed no hard feelings. Skywalker had a last message for our people.

"Through television," said Skywalker, "we finally understand 'kill.' Is that why your people will not return our explorers? What has happened, has happened. Please, explain our need and our acceptance of the past. We will wait for the bodies. Otherwise, our garden will be unbalanced forever."

Bookerman met my eyes and frowned. I asked the Hummers to send Fellini on ahead.

I don't know if Skywalker would have agreed to give us the equipment if he'd understood the risk to Bookerman and me. Washington should be grateful. Fifty-year-old bodies for a new set of gadgets.

This cell is far smaller than the room on the spaceship. 'Course, there were three of us there. Here, I'm alone. But then, I've been alone for a long time. Forever. I know you tried to contact me since Dad's funeral. Did you know he had his first stroke while I was at church listening to the priest talk about loaves and fishes? "There were four thousand people there, not counting the women and children." I wanted to be counted.

You don't know how much Dad depended on me after you went into the ministry. When Mom died, he lost interest in church, in clubs, even in fishing. Nothing mattered. I'd ask him over and over what I could do to help. He'd just shrug.

I had to at least give him the burial he wanted. He said he'd felt so cold since Mom died. Just once, he wanted to be warm again. When that old priest started going on about cremation flaunted God's laws…I know, I know, he was a dinosaur. It wasn't just that. It was a lot of things.

Even when I was a kid, I felt alone. Like everyone else was in a play and I was the only one who knew it was just a script. I used to think that if I left the church, I'd be terrified at death. Beg for a priest and Last Rites. So far, I feel mostly relief. You see, this chapter's over, and I don't have to be able to explain it after all. There won't be a test.

I feel bad about Bookerman, though. I was the one to suggest it. I don't think he would have done it on his own, but he went along. We both knew Washington was never going to release the bodies. Bookerman got us past security on the way in, but he was killed on the way out. He had the oddest look, like he'd ordered steak and gotten hamburger. The Hummers were horrified. Skywalker never would have allowed us to steal the bodies if he'd known what could happen.

I guess you heard their last message. I showed them how to use the satellites so everyone would get it. "May your garden be harmonious." High hopes.

They didn't let me attend his funeral. I wanted to try out what the aliens do at their wakes. On little paper flowers, they write down any hard feelings or unresolved resentments they feel toward the dead. They mulch them in with the body while they chant. "Forgive. Accept. Understand." The pains are buried so that the joys can be remembered clearly. I didn't have much to bury about Bookerman though.

I have one last request, Peter. I've never asked for your forgiveness. I want you to pray for me now. *Come close. I want to whisper. Keep praying. Louder. So the guards can't hear me. I know you'd have given it easily. I'm asking for something harder. Your trust.* Bless me, Father, for I have sinned. It has been many a long year since my last confession.

Skywalker learned about my arrest and tried to communicate with the MPs. His body shell didn't work in earth's gravity. Aliens don't handle bullets any better than humans. Somehow, Doc and Bashful retrieved his body. I guess they're learning. They took Skywalker home immediately for germination.

*I never expected to see any of them again. I don't know how Doc got past the sensors, the cameras, and the guards in a military prison. He seemed to know I wouldn't leave with him. I **am** a traitor and I accept my sentence.*

Doc came last night. Even after what happened to Skywalker two years ago, he risked his life to bring me something. Left his beautiful planet, perhaps forever. Faced unimagined violence. Mind you, they were prepared this time.

Look in my hand. Recognize them? The same seeds that were in the jam. Skywalker's seeds. I mixed them in. Insurance. I couldn't get them out, except through you. They'll search you. This was the only way. I'll swallow these, but I'm not sure if they'll survive the execution or the autopsy. You're my backup.

*Doc says the seed's shells are resilient. They have to be soaked in vinegar before sowing. Yours **will** survive.*

I want you to germilive my body. They'll expect you to claim it. Cremate me. Dig my ashes into a corner of your garden and add the seeds. Doc promised to come in two seasons for a packet. Be sure you have them ready. I explained how he could find you. Keep some or give him all of them; I don't much care. As long as I get to be part of the garden.

Skywalker, me, and millions of Hummers. Imagine the bouquet.

The End.

The Eighteenth

Vow

They stand in motionless silence, as decreed. Skins of black, white, yellow, red, and grey; poxed, mottled, tattooed, and artiskinned. All sizes, shapes, ages, and genders. There are few people but more variety since the last Great Plague and the Fifth Supremacy War. They wait to be chosen. At least the Aztec's captives struggled on their way to the altar.

There will be seven tests. To win the secrets of Mara, most powerful, death seems to them a fair risk. Mara, evil incarnate. The great seducer demon. But I participate for another reason.

No one recognizes me, yet I have met them in times of war, peace, and disease; in places of sand, rain, snow, and nuclear fallout. They look into my face but do not see. The world has forgotten me. I breathe their scents of smoke and beer, incense and flowers, oil and animal. Do I smell of the holy river or sweet rain?

Seven are chosen. It is time. We follow Mara into his fortress. The roll of this wheel has no beginning and no ending.[i]

* * * * *

As each competitor dies, we absorb their powers. The last survivor will have all. Seven centuries ago, Mara offered this contest. He has soured the earth ever since.

Even if my bones are crushed, I am grateful.[ii]

The competitor's shoes are the color of rust by the time there are only five left. I wash my bare feet nightly and chant for the dead. Three gone, five living, Yade, Wolfe, Leister, Adail, and myself. Although Mara will allow no wizardry but what he demands, only one gives his true name. In the way of magic, a name can be used to gain access to another's weakness, but if they called my name, it would be different.

We are fed only at nightfall. Liester tears his meat into thin strips with his bony fingers, watching everyone with his red-veined eyes. Wolfe devours his meat as though the flesh contained the secrets of the universe. Yade washes down each bite with ale. I express my gratitude for the plants given.

Mara keeps us separated at night, in case we have our own ideas of elimination. Each sleeps and studies in a windowless bombproof vault, Mara's defense against the Supremacy Wars. I can sense the others. Yade finds it difficult. His Spartan-like body wants to race and sweat and scream. Wolfe aches to battle. Whenever I miss the kiss of wind, I face the wall and meditate. The others search without, not knowing all is within.

The sterile darkness is unlike the vibrant caves in which I taught long ago. It is odorless, void, but not my void. Yet, I remember, wherever there is light, there is shadow; wherever there is white there is black.[liii]

Mara is a disembodied voice. We are kept in separate vaults, summoned as a group at the times for testing. Our next challenge is to remove the heart of a calf, yet not kill it. Much blood is spilled; all but one manages to keep their animal alive, bleating in terror. I am sickened by my action, but try to bring no pain. The animal is unaware of its artificial heart which will long outlast its living tissue. Leister snickers at my mundane response, but I have always disdained unnecessary miracles. Adail, the Moorish woman, dies as did her calf. Mara gives the calf Adail's heart and brings it back to life. He is not without a twisted sense of karma.

As we pass through the trials, Mara becomes more accessible: a shadow, a scent. Some grotesque reward for surviving?

Yade is the next to die. Poor fellow allows himself to yearn. Mara sends images from the nineteenth century: green spaces, untainted beauty, and purity. The fire of desire weakens Yade. He cannot concentrate on the Test of the Worm. He believes it is an undignified way for a man to fail, distracted by a dream. I could have told him he travels the path of illusion with legions. The mucus adds a new color to the shoes. I offer gratitude for clean water to bathe. My ojuzu beads are sticky and need to be rethreaded.

There is grudging respect in Mara's voice now that there are only three competitors remaining. Leister assesses me differently too. They all know it has nothing to do with size, but my delicate frame and soft features often mislead others. With my hair in a twisted top-knot, I seem even more fragile.

Wolfe is reckless enough to turn on Mara when he fumbles during the next test. The fire of anger is his undoing. We are "entertained" during our evening meal. Mara has the power to duplicate and is inspired by Vlad the Impaler. Wolfe dies around us in gruesome and agonizing varieties, each clone feeling the pain of the other as well as his own. No one else sees the irony of one as all and all as one. Should I be next, I will accept without pause. Death is sūnyatā.

Leister steps on my foot in leaving. His shoes are spiked, but his smirk fades when he sees there is no mark in the flesh. His eyes narrow.

Victory breeds hatred; the defeated live in pain. The peaceful live happily, giving up victory and defeat.[iv] I bow and leave for my vault. Tomorrow, only one will leave.

* * * * *

What cost passion? Leister would have won but for the break in concentration. The fire of lust is his undoing.

Mara has fooled him with an illusion, a woman of hideous beauty. A memory not experienced.

Of all the worldy passions, lust is the most intense. All other worldy passions seem to follow in its train. Lust is a viper hiding in a flower garden; it poisons those who come in search only of beauty. Lust is a vine that climbs a tree and spreads over the branches until the tree is strangled.[v]

I touch Leister's forehead.

"So," he says, "I am to die next. Why me?"

"You are like a village woman I once knew," I reply. "When her only child died of a fever on his threshold to manhood, she was unbalanced by grief. She begged me to restore her son's life."

"Did you?" Leister's voice is hopeful.

"I said if she could bring me a handful of poppy seeds from a village home that had not been touched by death, I would. She pounded on every door and was answered with compassion, yet the answer was always the same. Every house had experienced loss—a parent, child, spouse, or sibling. Finally, she returned empty-handed. She understood and accepted."

"And then?"

Mara's coldness enters the room. I know he has been listening.

"I helped her cremate him," I reply.

"Would you do the same for me?" asks Leister.

Mara appears in bodily form, growls and blasts him into motes of charcoal.

* * * * *

Mara sits across from me during the meal. I can see him clearly now; he has adopted a familiar shape. He is small and slight, with delicate features, his hair in a twisted top-knot, and 108 beads on his wrist. His eyes are blue and his skin olive. Is this tribute, or mockery? No matter.

"Is Sid short for Sidney or Sidden?" Mara asks.

"Both/neither," I reply.

He grins, "Your true name? And perhaps your true face?"

"One form of many. Like yours?" I say and reshape into a crimson-skinned devil with horns and a forked tail, then into a sky god.

"You think?" Mara laughs and slaps my shoulder. "It will be almost sad to kill you. I have not had a challenger like you in centuries. Unwavering. Single-minded."

"Perhaps I could spare you the discomfort," I offer.

"Sorry no. I couldn't possibly let a rival free with the power of seven. You know how it is. I never know who might turn on me."

I shake my head.

He frowns. "You take no joy in the defeat of your enemies?"

"I have no enemies."

"*Had*," he corrects with a wave of his finger.

"They are still here." I touch my head and heart.

"Soon they, and you, will dwell within me. I will have immeasurable power."

"Power is a fool's refuge. To conquer oneself is a greater victory than to conquer thousands in battle."

Mara stands. The food and the table disappear. He places his hand on my cool forehead and concentrates. Suddenly he pulls it back. His eyes widen. "Who are you?"

"Simply Sid."

His body changes into that of Yade. He rips the robe from my shoulders, tears the clothes. "A woman! Impossible."

"Merely improbable." I piece together my clothing and get dressed.

Mara laughs. "Absorbing women gives me vertigo, but so be it."

He places both hands on my head. I draw Yade, Wolfe, Leister, and the others into a circle of light. Mara jerks back his hand and hisses.

"What is this?"

"Non-duality," I respond.

He snarls and slams his hands back on my head. The world sways, then swirls. It crashes and roars. We follow it, the eight contestants. We ride the turmoil like a leaf in the rapids. Mara pulls away, gasping. Slowly, he reforms into a tall, thin man with black shoulder-length hair.

"I have all eternity to subdue you," he says.

"Could we not settle it in a fair contest?"

Mara grins at the word "fair." He wonders what I am up to but can see no alternative. Besides, he has no qualms about cheating. "Agreed."

"I choose the test this time."

He hisses.

"Surely your magic can match mine?" I continue as he growls. "I will give you a fair deal."

His eyes light up and he quiets.

"I will go first. You must copy my task exactly. If you do, you win."

"Just copy it? Not better it or undo it?"

"That's right. But it must be precisely the same and there must be no alteration of history."

He pauses, then nods. "Deal. The winner devours the loser and all her powers."

"No."

"What then?" His voice rises with impatience. The room warms.

"The winner chooses the final test. In this test it will be winner take all. That way you will have a chance to choose the final challenge. If you win the first one."

"Agreed."

* * * * *

He calls me a cheat because the first test was not magical. I dare to differ. There is enchantment in every rock, every drop of water, and every stick.

I choose the Ganges, for sentimental reasons. I throw a small branch of the sala tree into the river. We watch it swirl slowly downstream. He is bewildered when I say, "Your turn."

He retrieves the branch and tosses it into the same spot. He ensures that it moves the same way. We watch it disappear around the bend.

"I don't get it," he says.

"That's right, you don't."

He frowns and crosses his arms. "Explain."

"It must be the same and there must be no alteration of history."

"Same branch. Same river. Same movements."

"No. The branch has changed between the time I threw it and you threw it. The river has changed. It is not the same water. The soil is disturbed. The creatures on its bed have moved, or died, or hatched between my throw and yours. Nothing is the same from one moment to the next. All is transcience. Anitya."

"Cheat." His eyes narrow and dark clouds form over the horizon.

My skin prickles.

"I know you," he says. His hair falls forward as he leans toward me. It is thick and glossy black. "I tried to tempt you under the Bo tree. Why a woman's body now?"

"For balance," I say. "It is time for this and much else to be balanced."

"Very well, Sid-Every Wish Fulfilled," he sneers. "You win this round. Give me the second test, but it must be totally unlike the first. I will copy nothing. And not non-duality tests."

"I'm not sure if you have the stamina for this one," I say.

He snarls.

"For one kalpa—the time it takes an angel's wing to wear down a rock that is forty Chinese miles on each side if it is brushed once every three years—we will test each other's endurance."

"One kalpa!"

"I know I can survive, but if it is too difficult for you—"

"I accept the challenge. Explain."

"During this time, we are not to grow, purchase, gather, hunt or obtain food by any method using our own skills. Instead, we must depend entirely on the charity of others. They cannot be coerced, tricked, or bribed. It must be given to us freely."

"You think no one will fill my begging bowl. You're probably right. Therefore, I demand an amendment. Neither of us are to let the people know who we are. We will be nameless."

Mara thought people would fill our bowls equally but, of course, karma cannot be denied. Mara is who he is, disguised or not. More than once he lies starving and I fill his bowl while he sleeps.

I watch him transform. At first it is all outward deception, putting on the false face, but in time, his karma changes as he welcomes the smiles as much as the food. I know the darkness within him is lifting.

One night, when he has travelled for days through a famine-stricken land, I stop again to fill his bowl. He wakes and grabs my arm."Why?"

"I have what you need."

I slip away as he bends to the bowl.

In time, he comes to count on me, knowing I will come when his bowl has been barren for too long. Each time, his question is the same, as is the answer.

Eventually, he stops asking. Then he tells me about a duck he has seen and how he had first thought of how delicious it would taste on a roasting spit. A hawk dove toward the bird and he inwardly cheered for its escape.

"Do you suppose I wanted the hawk to starve, like me?" He brushes back his dark hair, now streaked with grey. "I am so tired."

"Life is suffering," I answer.

* * * * *

In the 24,000[th] year, the angel's wing brushes the rock. Mara speaks. "I am aging. Even if I win this battle, I will never be the same. My strength is depleted."

"To see impermanent things as permanent is the truth of the cause of suffering," I explain. "Anitya."[vi]

I hide a biscuit in his belongings. Coming upon him days later, I ask him if he has enjoyed it.

"What are you talking about? I am starved!" he shouts.

I show him how he has been carrying what he needed without knowing it. He devours the biscuit in three bites. "That is a cruel trick." He groans.

"You are the one who is unconscious of what you already carry," I answer. I don't think he understands.

* * * * *

In the 2,970,000th year he asks, "Why is it you seem not to suffer by this trial as I do? How can you exist in this miserable world and still smile?"

In compassion, I reply, "I see things as they are, in the pure light. Have you not watched the changes go by, heard the futile cries of protest? I live not in this world, but in Ojodo."

I watch his travels. One especially harsh winter, he takes shelter in a destitute village. Food runs low.

"Why do you keep these useless old people?" he cries to the villagers. "They don't work, yet they eat? You should bring them to the mountain and leave them. Then we will have more food and the predators will be distracted."

The people are swayed by his words. They bring the elders up the rough mountain trail. One young man carried his mother on his back. As they travel, she reaches out and snaps off branches.

"Stop that!" orders Mara. He warns the young man, "You mustn't let her mark the trail. If she returns, you will just have to carry her away again."

"I am not going to return to the village," says the mother. "I am marking the trail so my son will not be lost on the way home."

The villagers are filled with shame at her words and take all the elders back to the village. Mara slinks off during the night.

* * * * *

In the 43,260,000th year, Mara cries out, "How? How is it possible to extinguish the pain?"

I take his hand. "Walk in my path. Eight simple steps will bring you to the cessation of suffering."

"I cannot move."

"One step at a time," I say. "We will start with right thoughts."

He shuffles to his feet and follows. Both our heads are now bare. "There are so few people left," he moans. "Why do you stay with me?"

"I made forty-eight vows," I reply. "You will help me to accomplish the eighteenth[vii], my last unfulfilled."

"I did not call you will a sincere heart," snaps Mara, his old fire returning.

"I know," I say. "There is still time. Call me Amida."

* * * * *

The angel's wing brushes, signaling the 856,581,000th year. There are fewer and fewer dwelling in the world of suffering Mara's bowl is often empty, as is mine. I teach him to chant, centering the self/not self and stilling the pain of hunger. I give him a string of 108 beads to remind him of possibilities. I train him to meditate, and the tears run down his weathered, aged face.

"I have forgotten the prize," he confides one day.

"It's all right," I reply. "I haven't. Do you trust me to reward you should you succeed?"

"Yes. Why do you do this?"

So, I tell the story of the father returning home from a trip to find his house on fire. It is one of my favorites and often misunderstood. His children were inside, and although he called, "Come out, there is a fire, you are in danger!" the children would not leave their toys. He knew there was little time before the fire would spread and consume them, so he shouted, "You don't need those old toys. I have brought you bigger and better ones. Come out to me." So the children left the building and were saved.

* * * * *

In the 5,669,999,999th year, Mara smiles. "The fire is weakening. I no longer burn for what belongs to another, strive for power, hold contempt for any sentient beings, and dwell on the desires of self. I see the rain fall, winds blow, plants mature, leaves die and be blown away. Am I a cause or a condition?"

"Your candle has been extinguished." I wipe a smudge of dirt from his cheek.

"I am old," he says.

"Yes."

"I am sick."

"Yes."

"I am going to die."

"Yes."

"I will dissolve and be blown away. Like the wind and the rain and the leaves. I will cease to exist." He sighs.

"You must be thirsty," I say. "Have this bowl of rice milk. It was given to me by a young maiden, the last of her kind."

"Only if you drink first," he responds.

"I have already, a long time ago." I hold it out to him. "Welcome to the Sangha."

Quietly, he lifts the bowl and swallows. He lowers the bowl to the earth and wipes his lips. His eyes widen. A tear flows down one weathered cheek. The year changes. One kalpa ends.

He whispers, "Amida, Amida, Amida. Am I dying?"

I step forward to enfold him. The eighth test is turned on its side. Eight is infinity. Seven plus one equals one. The eight/one move into the light of the Pure Land. We are black, white, yellow, red, and grey; poxed, mottled, tattooed, and artiskinned. All sizes, shapes, ages, and genders. The roll of this wheel has no beginning and no ending.

"Yes," I say, stroking his wrinkled hand.

"Who are you?" he asks.

"Siddhartha/Dharmakara/Sakyamuni Buddha/Amida/Shinran/Leister/Mara and more," I reply. "I am transfiguration and incarnation. I am the sky, the stars, and the spaces between. I am nature, energy, mind and personality."

"Namu Amida Butsu," he calls with a sincere heart.

I stretch my left hand toward him and my right toward the heavens. "But now, thanks to you, I am Maitreya Bodhisattva, and so are you. The future Buddha. Buddha of Infinite Light and Boundless Life!"

He shimmers, shifts, and flows into me. The light surrounds us, enters us, is us. We/I am Englightenment.

The End.

Okasan

Shonogo, the skilled and honorable Samurai lizard,

walked two steps past the lotus pond. A peasant paused in

his rice fathering to bow. Shonogo bowed in return.

The Samurai reached the bamboo bridge just as a

Ninja leaped out from behind a pippala tree. Shonogo

swung his sword. The Ninja transformed into treasure.

"Mitchell," said Noreen. "Shut off the computer and

go out to play. Don't go near McCormick's yard. That

horrid pit bull is tied outside again."

Mitchell sighed, passed his hand over his brush cut,

and shut down the system. Whever he felt the link clearing,

Okasan would break it.

At lunch time, Mitchell raced in for a sandwich and two glasses of milk. "Please don't come into the back yard until I tell you," he told his mother.

She nodded absently.

At supper, Mitchell wolfed down his food. "Come outside as soon as you're done," he said.

"I'm done now," Noreen said as she pushed her plate away.

He led her out the back door.

"A sand garden," he explained with a wave of his hand. "Now you won't be upset when the flowers don't grow the way you like."

Noreen gasped.

"See the way the sand is raked into waves," said Mitchell. "If you sit and watch, it will make you feel good."

"Where did you get the sand?" shrieked his mother. She dug her fingers into his small shoulder.

"From the old sandbox."

"Just because you don't play in the sand anymore is no reason to throw it around the yard."

"I was careful not to get any on the grass. There are seven big rocks, but no matter where you stand, you can only see six. That was hard to do. Look, Okasan."

Go to your room. Your father will be home in an hour and then we'll see."

"Life is suffering," muttered Mitchell.

* * * * *

"What is wrong with that child?" asked Noreen.

"He's just being a kid," said her husband, Alex.

"All I can say is, thank God we only have one."

"Noreen, be fair. Mitchell is a good boy. You're much too hard on him."

"How would you know? You're never here."

"Come on, I've taken him on trips whenever I could. I give you afternoons to yourself when I'm home. Mitchell and I get along fine together."

Noreen huffed. "That's because you let him do whatever he wants."

Alex leaned back in his chair and undid his tie. "Maybe you should think about getting a job. Getting out more might do you some good."

"You promised I could stay home and paint," said Noreen.

"When's the last time you picked up a brush?"

Noreen crossed her arms. "Mitchell ruined the garden and now you're criticizing me."

"You never seem to be happy anymore."

"What's to be happy about an eleven year old who ruins my things and calls me stupid names? He's so defiant, I find myself fighting not to become enraged."

"What names?" asked Alex.

"Okasan. Why is he being rude like that?"

"It's just some kind of Ninja phase. I'll talk to him about it."

Noreen nodded and unfolded her arms. "And the garden?"

"I'll tell him no more landscaping without your permission."

"Very funny, Alex. The soil is ruined now."

Alex smirked. "It was a weed pit to begin with. It can't look any worse."

Noreen flung back her chair and ran to the bedroom. The lock clicked into place.

* * * * *

Noreen poised her brush over the paper. She had been painting, just nothing she wanted to show Alex. She did not want him to question the images. She wasn't sure where they came from.

Once, she'd begun by painting a landscape with a snow-capped mountain in the distance, and ended with a picture of twisted, broken flowers and shrubs. Another time, she'd discovered Mitchell's face hidden in the trunk of a blighted peach tree. His mouth was open in a soundless scream. She had suddenly felt ill. She ran to the sink, shoved aside the jars and brushes, and vomited in an angry gush. A third time, a skeletal hand and foot appeared in the middle of a bouquet of cherry blossoms.

* * * * *

Noreen watched the boys through the front window. Mitchell and his friend Joseph shouted and taunted each other in a boisterous game of tag. Mitchell might not fit comfortably into her life, but he had no trouble with his peers. His speed and coordination guaranteed he was among the first chosen for any team sport.

Joseph was a new friend, recently arrived from Croatia. He was still learning to speak English, but tag was a game that crossed all barriers.

McCormick's pit bull barked wildly. Joseph looked up, stumbled over the curbing and fell onto the asphalt driveway. Immediately, Mitchell ran to his side and helped him up. Joseph clutched his knee as they staggered toward the house. As Noreen held the door for them, Joseph limped inside, fighting back tears.

"Joseph needs a bandaid," said Mitchell.

After the first aid was complete, Noreen provided the boys with chocolate milk and peanut butter cookies at the kitchen table.

"Have some fruit from the bowl," she said to Joseph.

"Thanks," he mumbled as he bit into a peach. "Good." He took another one from the bowl and held it out to Mitchell.

Mitchell paled and shook his head. "I can't eat peaches."

"Why?"

"Just the smell makes my stomach hurt. I HATE peaches."

"Well, take an apple then," snapped Noreen. She never understood why it felt as though Mitchell's allergy was her fault.

* * * * *

Shonogo offered his treasure to the poor man.

The peasant shouted, "Life is but an illusion!" and tore off his disguise. The deceptive Ninja threw his star.

Shonogo was prepared. He sliced down with his sword, deflecting the star, push-kicked the Ninja, and then ended his miserable life.

"Mitchell Leland. Are you playing that awful game again. Give me the laptop," demanded Noreen. "You have lost this computer until further notice."

"But it helps me focus."

"I told you not to play that game so much. Every time I turn around, you're at it. Hand it over."

"Yes, Okasan."

"I told you not to say that. Can't you ever be obedient?"

"Yes, mother," Mitchell bowed and went into his room. Noreen watched his erect walk. She wrapped the cord around the computer and put it into the top shelf of the closet. Her hands shook. Quietly, she went to Mitchell's room and peered through the partially open door.

Mitchell stood in front of a small red plasticine figure on his mostly empty dresser top. The clay was finely sculptured into a man wearing a top-knot and sitting in the lotus position. A twig with white flowers was stuck into a ball of plasticine beside it.

He spoke to the figure. "I am one of two faces. One of the jeans, and one of the belt. Which is real?"

Noreen felt cold prickles traveling up her spine.

"Okasan does not understand. She lives in the small mind, as she did before—"

"Mitchell."

"Maybe it would be better if you went to play outside."

Mitchell turned and looked her eyes. His seemed very old.

"Go on," said Noreen.

After Mitchell left, Noreen threw the flowered twig in the trash and crushed the plasticine man. She rolled the clay around and around, squeezing and rubbing it smooth. She shoved the plasticine into the ice cream bucket in the bottom of her son's closet and shut the door.

In the kitchen, she washed her hands over and over, trying to rid them of the oily feeling.

"Look, Mom."

Noreen jumped.

Mitchell stood in the doorway with a small bunch of pink bleeding hearts in his hand. "I found them growing through the fence. Can I have a vase?"

"I'll get it."

He plucked off the leaves until there were only two left.

"That's awfully bare," said Noreen.

"I like it," said Mitchell as he arranged them. The flowers looked starkly balanced as he carried them into his room. A moment later, Noreen heard the closet door open and the peeling sound of the lid of the ice cream bucket.

* * * * *

The next week Noreen decided to meet Mitchell after school. She'd fallen asleep on the couch and had the strangest dream. Mitchell was dressed as a Samurai. She'd torn the uniform from his body, striking him over and over as she did. She needed to see him in his Rough Rider jeans and Blue Bomber jacket.

She walked on the opposite side of the street from McCormick's. The dog was barking so loudly, she didn't hear the shouting boys until she saw them.

Joseph was sitting on the ground, his face smeared with blood. Four boys circled Mitchell, kicking and punching.

"Should have minded your own business, Leland," yelled the largest boy.

"I'm warning you, Jeff!" said Mitchell.

The big boy laughed and kicked at Joseph. Mitchell moved in a blur and Jeff crashed into the pavement. Mitchell spun and axe-kicked another child in the stomach, whirled again and reversed punched the third boy in the jaw. He grabbed the arm of a boy in a Montreal Canadiens sweatshirt and forced him to the ground. Jeff attacked from behind. There was a loud snap and the Montreal Canadiens fan screamed. Noreen reached the group.

"Stop!" she screamed. "Stop this right now!"

The boy holding his stomach whimpered and stumbled away. The one Mitchell had punched in the jaw ran, Nikes slapping.

Jeff muttered to Mitchell, "We're not finished with you yet."

"Take your brother and get out of here," said Mitchell.

Jeff glared.

"Do it," ordered Noreen. "Mitchell's father and I will be talking to your parents."

They took Joseph home. His mother thanked them and took him quickly inside.

After Mitchell had cleaned up, Noreen questioned him in the kitchen.

"They were beating up on Joseph," said Mitchell. "For no good reason. I must protect those who are weaker than myself."

"What?"

"It was four to one."

"I just hate to see you fighting. It's so dangerous."

"Is that why you never come to my karate classes?" asked Mitchell, his eyes narrowing. "Not even the tournaments."

Noreen was relieved when Alex arrived home then, interrupting the uncomfortable questioning.

* * * * *

The Samurai was ready. Their peasant disguise would not fool him again. When the third Ninja jumped from behind the tree, Shonogo did not hesitate. Soon, the bodies of the three cowards lay scattered on the path.

He drew his sword when the next peasant approached. In terror, the poor man dropped his possessions and fled. Shonogo was ashamed. He had attacked an innocent man. He fell to his knees.

"I have lost face," he cried. "My karma is a stone on my heart." He plunged his sword into his stomach. The funeral music sounded.

Shonogo began his second life, stronger and wiser. This time he would succeed.

"Does your father know you're using his computer?" demanded Noreen.

"Yes, I asked him if I could use it."

"Did you tell him why you didn't have your own?"

Mitchell shook his head.

"Shut it down, now!"

Mitchell did.

"Let me make this perfectly clear. You are banned from any and all computers. Got it?"

"Yes, Okasan."

"Mom! You drive me crazy with this Jap stuff."

Mitchell narrowed his eyes. "Now you sound like those bullies. Are you are racist too?"

"Of course not," she shouted, then paused, took a deep breath and lowered her voice. "You are not Japanese.

You are not a warrior or . . . anything. You're a WASP, for God's sake."

"Illusion," said Mitchell.

"You don't even know what that means."

"Neither do you." He crossed his arms and raised his chin.

Noreen pointed her finger. "Stop parroting this nonsense. You are Mitchell Leland, my eleven year old son, an ordinary boy, and you will behave the way I believe is appropriate. You will obey me."

"This time I must find my own way."

Noreen grabbed his shoulders and shook him. "Shut up. You're talking like a lunatic. I am your mother. You will do as I say. I SAY!"

"Why don't you just feed me some peaches? You know you want to."

Smack! Noreen's slap left a red mark on his pale cheek. She stepped back, horrified, then turned and ran into the bathroom to vomit.

* * * * *

Four days after the schoolyard fight, at 3:45 .m., McCormick's pit bull broke his chain. He headed straight for Leland's yard where Mitchell and Joseph were perusing comics on the front step.

The Samurai heard the dragon before he saw it. He had only his traveling bag for a weapon, but he did not hesitate.

Noreen couldn't believe Joseph could shriek like that. Looking through the kitchen window, she saw him on the sidewalk between the dog's front paws. Its jaw was lathered in saliva and blood. Noreen yanked the cupboard drawer so hard, its contents crashed to the floor. She grabbed the bread knife and tore out the door.

"Get him to safety," shouted the Samurai as he leapt onto the dragon's back and clenched the strap of his traveling bag into its throat.

Noreen pulled Joseph to the side, and then plunged the knife into the pit bulls stocky chest, once, twice, the blade clanking on thick bone. Joseph lay on the grass, whimpering. The dog collapsed.

"I'm alright," said Mitchell. "Joseph's bleeding bad."

Noreen gagged at the sight of the child's torn arm. "You saved him," she said.

"I was meant to."

Noreen bit her lip. "I'm sorry I never came to see your tournaments." She shook her head, as if to clear her thoughts, and then helped Joseph indoors.

"She understands," said the Samurai. "This time, perhaps she will let me be who I must be."

He smiled widely, releasing his grip on the dragon. He would speak with his honored mother. She would grow to love him as he was. There would be no peaches in their future.

The dragon sensed the Samurai's distraction. He lunged.

* * * * *

"It's not your fault," said Alex. "No one would have suspected the dog would rally."

Alex stroked Noreen's hair as she sobbed against his shoulder in the hospital bereavement room.

"How could such a little boy have so much courage?" whispered Noreen.

She kept his room virtually unchanged after Mitchell's death. Alex did not feel this was healthy for either of them, but he tread softly. Noreen had terrible recurring nightmares.

She dreamt herself screaming at Mitchell, insisting that he join her brother in the family pottery business. Odd, since she had no brother.

Mitchell shook his head. "I must follow my own path."

She slapped him hard, over and over. "You will not disobey me. You will not become the Shogun's pawn. You will not throw away the life I gave you for strangers." She yanked his hair. "You will stay with your family, grow up, and care for us in our old age. You are our only son. I will kill you before I let you desert us. I will kill you and bury you in the garden when only the worms will know."

Sometimes she woke to the smell of peaches, strangely underlaid with a chemical scent.

She spent more time in Mitchell's room, trying to solve the puzzle of his life.

"I know you think I'm stuck in the denial stage," said Noreen when Alex tried to discard the plasticine figure. "Maybe I am, but I just can't bear to throw out his things. Would it be alright if I just packed them in boxes? Could we keep them in the basement?"

"I'll help you pack them," said Alex.

* * * * *

Less than a year later, Alex came home to find Noreen going through the boxes. His brow creased.

"Don't worry," said Noreen. "I'm just looking for his wall-hanging. I thought it might be nice for the nursery."

Alex's eyes widened as Noreen smiled hesitantly.

"Perhaps a daughter this time." He hugged her tightly. "Someone you can be close to."

"No matter. Whoever it is, I will try so hard, so very hard, to love them just as they are."

* * * * *

The Leland baby's first cries rang through the maternity ward like a gong. Alex's work took him out of town more often. The pregnancy and birth had been very difficult and Noreen was completely depleted. The only solution was a nanny. Alex obtained a name from a business acquaintance.

"Mrs. Schmidt seems just what we're looking for," he told Noreen.

Alex greeted Mrs. Schmidt at the door, while Noreen tried to calm the baby in the nursery.

Noreen paced, jiggled, and made soothing noises. "You'll scare her off, darling."

The red-faced squalling continued. She could faintly hear her husband's voice, but not the nanny's. Her head pounded, but she was determined to be patient. A moment later, Alex opened the door.

"She wants to see the baby. She seems very quiet and calm."

"How will she cope with this little beasty?"

"Let's find out." Alex took the baby.

As Noreen washed her hands, she listened. She could hear her husband occasionally and a different sing-song voice. No crying.

She paused at the living room entrance. Mrs. Schmidt sat with the baby on her lap. She was bent over, humming softly. She was a small woman with dark hair. Noreen walked across the room.

"How do you do? I'm Noreen Leland."

The woman looked up. "So happy to meet you," responded Mrs. Schmidt in a heavy Japanese accent.

Noreen was startled by the depth of the woman's Asian black eyes. "Mrs. Schmidt. That's a German name, isn't it?"

"*So desu.*" The nanny nodded. "My husband was German, but I am from Kyoto."

"I hope you can handle a colicky baby," said Noreen. "He seems as though he was born with a stomach ache."

"This too will change. Nothing is permanent."

Noreen smiled, comforted by the remark.

* * * * *

Noreen pauses at the sand-filled flower bed. She decided to keep it the way it was. Its serenity cures headaches. Sometimes she sits here and considers the advice Obachan, as they call Mrs. Schmidt, offers in small doses. One that is difficult to achieve is the goal of right effort, "to direct our efforts incessantly to the overcoming of ignorance and selfish desires."

The wind has altered the rake lines into less rigid patterns, but still there is order to the broken waves. She thinks of Mitchell. His memory, like the waves, seems softer. It is the law of impermanence that intrigues Noreen most, offering both despair and freedom.

She gathers the half-wild bleeding hearts that grow through the fence, plucks off most of the leaves, and brings them into her workroom. She gathers her painting materials.

Noreen poises the brush above the canvas. The shading isn't right. She walks to the table and turns the vase, examining the flower shadows on the cherry wood surface. She nods, satisfied, and returns to the easel. All her landscapes and floral arrangements now hold healthy, balanced flowers.

Thomas enters. "I like that," he announces in his bright childish voice.

Noreen smiles. "Do you want to paint, son?"

Thomas nods. Noreen picks up a peach beside her easel and bites into it. Thomas shudders as the juice trickles down her skin. She wipes her chin and lays the peach on the table. Thomas stares at it for a moment, lips pressed tightly together, and then turns away.

"What will you paint today?" asks Noreen.

"I don't know."

"How about a kitty? Or a puppy?"

"I HATE dogs," says Thomas.

Noreen studies his serious expression. She wonders if she has let something slip. "Some dogs are nice. I had a poodle when I was a little girl. He was sweet."

"Okay. I won't hate poodles, but I still hate mean dogs."

"That's your choice, honey. You can decide."

"Can I?" asks Thomas.

"Can you what?"

"Decide things for myself."

"Sure, unless you're too little."

"When I grow up?"

"Of course."

Thomas smiles, his gappy grin tugs at her heart.

"Here," she says, passing him a brush. "Make your picture." She clips a large sheet of paper on a small easel.

She is amazed at how quiet Thomas is when he paints. The mess doesn't bother her. Mrs. Schmidt will scrub away any stains on his clothes. Noreen had considered letting Mrs. Schmidt go once Thomas reached school age, but she knew she would miss the woman as much as Thomas, for many reasons. Instead, they offered her room and board in exchange for a lower wage.

"Want some red paint?" Noreen asks.

"No, yellow. Yellow is my favorite color."

Noreen returns to her still life. She'll have no trouble selling this watercolor. The gallery has been pressuring her for more. They sell as fast as she can create them.

Thomas dips his brush. Down the page, he carefully draws a J and a box, followed by two hammock shaped lines, a hook, and a tent. Noreen immerses herself in the shadow of a petal. Thomas finishes off a page with a flourish of yellow waves around the border of the paper.

"I'm done," he says. "I made a story."

"Did you? Leave it there to dry so you can read it to Daddy and I at supper."

Thomas nods. Noreen goes to the sink and rinses her brush. The splashing water veils Thomas' small voice as he reads aloud. He follows the golden lines arranged into calligraphic figures down the page.

"Daddy goes to work. Thomas gets big. He grows up. He is smart. He is good. He can walk his own path. Okasan learns."

The End.

If you enjoyed these stories, perhaps you will enjoy more of Bonnie's work. Check here for what's available.

http://www.amazon.com/s/ref=sr_tc_2_0?rh=i%3Astripbooks%2Ck%3ABonnie+Ferrante&keywords=Bonnie+Ferrante&ie=UTF8&qid=1333832275&sr=1-2-ent&field-contributor_id=B007P7LFYG

Visit her on Facebook – Bonnie Ferrante

Tweet her on Twitter – BonnieFerrante

Visit her website -

http://my.tbaytel.net/bonnieheather/index.htm

Or her blog - http://steppingquietly.blogspot.com/

Or her Youtube channel -

http://www.youtube.com/user/Bonnie0904/videos

---

[i] *The Teaching of the Buddha,* Human Defilements.

[ii] Shinran Shonen.

[iii] *The Teaching of the Buddha*, The Theory of Mind Only.

[iv] *The Teaching of the Buddha*, Dhammapada.

[v] *The Teaching of the Buddha,* Human Defilements.

[vi] *The Teaching of the Buddha*, Transitoriness or Impermanence. "ALL existence and phenomena in this world are changing constantly and do not remain the same for even a single moment. Everything has to die or end some day in the future, and such a prospect is the very cause of suffering. This concept should not, however, be interpreted only from a pessimistic or nihilistic viewpoint, because both advancement and reproduction are also manifestations of this constant change.

[vii] In the Larger Sukhavâtivyûha Sutra, Sakyamuni Buddha tells of the vows made by Dharmaka. – Though I attain Buddhahood, I shall never be complete until people everywhere determine to attain Englightenment, practice virtues, wish to be born in my land with sincerity; thus, I shall appear at the moment of their death with a great company of Bodhisattvas to welcome them into my Pure Land. Though I attain Buddhahood, I shall never be complete until people everywhere, hearing my name, gain right ideas about life and death, and gain that perfect wisdom that will keep their minds pure and tranquil in the midst of the world's greed and suffering.

About the Author

Learn more about Bonnie online at http://my.tbaytel.net/bonnieheather/index.htm or checkout her author page on Amazon or Goodreads. Follow her (Bonnie Ferrante - Author) on Facebook, on Twitter (Bonnie Ferrante) or Pinterest.

Please consider leaving a positive review on Amazon or Goodreads.

www.ingramcontent.com/pod-product-compliance
Lightning Source LLC
Chambersburg PA
CBHW070645130626
46555CB00006B/2709